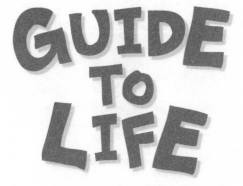

GUIDE TO LIFE

Written by Scott Peterson

"Happy Birthday, Perry!" comic insert—Writer: Scott Peterson; Pencils: John Green;
Inks: Mike DeCarlo; Colors: Garry Black; Letters: Michael Stewart

"That's Snow Man, That's a Monster!" comic insert—Writer: Scott Peterson;
Pencils & Inks: Eric Jones; Colors: Emily Kanalz; Letters: Michael Stewart

Based on the series created by
Dan Povenmire & Jeff "Swampy" Marsh

Copyright © 2011 Disney Enterprises, Inc.

Printed in the United States of America
Second Edition, September 2020
1 3 5 7 9 10 8 6 4 2
FAC-034274-20199
ISBN 978-1-368-06573-3

For more Disney Press fun, visit www.disneybooks.com

GUIDE TO LIFE

By *Phineas & Ferb*

DISNEP PRESS

Los Angeles • New York

FOREWORD

Hey! Phineas and Ferb here. "Whatcha doin'?" is what our friend Isabella asks us every time she comes over to our house. And now it's the question we are asking **you**. Whatcha doin' with your life? Are you making the most of every day? Did you invent a time machine yesterday? Or build a massive ski slope in your backyard? If not, then this book is for you!

You hold in your hands our *Guide to Life*. Inside, we'll offer you time-tested advice and suggestions to make the most out of your life—the Phineas and Ferb way!

We've also thrown in some cool, fun activities, because if you know us, creativity is the key to everything!

And now, we present you with our philosophy on life, which can be summed up in three simple statements:

• **Seize the day.**

• **If you dream it, you can do it. We thought it would be totally cool to have a giant marine aquarium in our backyard. So we built one!**

• **There is no problem that can't be solved with duct tape and peanut butter.**

WHO ARE WE?

If you're about to use our guide to life, it's essential that you know who we are.

You wouldn't want to follow the advice of someone you didn't really know, would you? We hope not! That wouldn't be very smart. And, if you don't mind us saying, you must be quite intelligent, since you went out and bought this book!

It is in this spirit that we present you with vital facts about us!

YOU DON'T LOOK THAT SMART TO ME.

THREE THINGS YOU SHOULD KNOW ABOUT PHINEAS:

▶ Best friend is his stepbrother, Ferb.

▶ Boredom is something that he will not stand for.

▶ Is an eternal optimist. His glass is not only half full— it's half full of root beer float!

PHINEAS BY THE NUMBERS:

Stairs to Bedroom: *12*

Shoe Size: *6*

Favorite Milk: *2%*

Things He's Gonna Do Today: *AT LEAST 1*

THREE THINGS YOU SHOULD KNOW ABOUT FERB:

▶ Can talk whenever he pleases, but sees himself as more of a man of action.

▶ Has a way with tools and can build anything from a time-traveling robot to a nuclear-powered kangaroo.

▶ Looks stunning in purple pants.

FERB ACROSS THE GLOBE:

Born: *ENGLAND*

Current Home: *DANVILLE*

Furthest Vacation: *MARS*

Favorite Spot: *HIS FAMILY'S BACKYARD*

THREE THINGS YOU SHOULD KNOW ABOUT CANDACE:

▶ Was the lead actress in *The Curse of the Princess Monster* (formerly known as *The Princess Sensibilities*).

▶ Is really good at limbo. Was even crowned "Queen Wahini" at Phineas and Ferb's backyard beach party.

▶ Can be just a little, tiny, sort of, kind of, teeny, eensy, weensy bit obsessive.

CANDACE FAVES:

Favorite Band: *TINY COWBOY*

Favorite Guy: *JEREMY . . . DUH!*

Favorite Phrase: *BUT, BUT, BUT . . .*

PLATYPUS FUN FACTS

Here are some real, true-life facts about platypuses (#1: some people say *platypi*) that we learned when we got our pet platypus, Perry.

▶ It's one of only two mammals to lay eggs. The other is the echidna, which is a spiny anteater!

▶ A platypus has no teeth. It puts rocks in its mouth along with its food and uses the rocks to crush the food. Weird!

▶ On that note, a platypus spends around twelve hours a day looking for food. Want to know why? Because it must eat at least one quarter of its body weight each day.

▶ A platypus swims with its eyes, ears, and nostrils shut, propelling itself forward with the help of its front feet. Its back feet are used to brake and steer—like with a car!

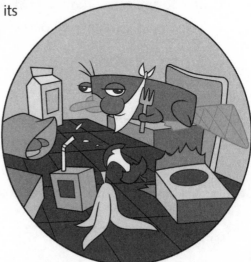

WHO ARE YOU?

Now that you know all about us, let's find out about you!

It's important to know who you are and what you like. This page will help you identify those things. It may even give you some inspiration for your next project . . . or your next snack!

What's your favorite . . .

Book? ....

Movie? ....

TV show? ....

Song? ....

Food? ....

Drink? ....

Pizza topping? ....

Animal? ....

Game? ....

Cartoon character? ....

Duck-billed secret agent? ....

MY FAVORITE SONG IS DEFINITELY NOT "THE EENSIE-WEENSIE SPIDER."

You know exactly what we look like. (And if you don't, just glance at the top left corner of this page!) Now we're curious to learn what you look like. Feel free to embellish yourself. Think your ears are too big? You can make them smaller—we won't know! Wish your eyelashes were ten feet long? Not sure why you'd want that, but go ahead and make them never-ending!

DRAW YOUR PICTURE HERE

What to Do If You Meet an Alien

Okay, now that we know a little about you, let's talk about something we love: aliens! Take it from us: meeting an alien is an exciting but tricky event. Here are five important things to do—and NOT do—when encountering an alien being.

1. Don't make any menacing, or non-menacing, gestures, such as moving quickly, moving slowly, raising your hands, lowering your hands, frowning, or smiling.

2. Don't just stand there, either.

3. If you try to initiate a handshake, don't shake anything until you are sure it's a hand.

4. Don't just talk about yourself—that's rude on any planet. Make sure to ask the alien questions.

5. Don't flap your arms like wings and run around in a circle singing "Pop Goes the Weasel." It's a long story. Just trust us.

Buford Van Stomm Presents

WOULD YOU RATHER?

Sometimes in life you gotta make choices. Like now. Pick one: Would you rather get chased by a mummy or caught in a storm of falling lawn gnomes?

HOW TO...
REUNITE A BAND

Sometimes the world is in danger. Sometimes a life is on the line. And sometimes you just have to get some ex–band members together for a concert. But how? Don't worry, we've got a foolproof method that works every time.

- Find the members. Use the Internet, old fan clubs, or check your local diner. They're probably ordering the used-to-be-a-rock-star special.

- Flatter them, build up their egos, and convince them that aging, former rock stars still matter.

- Sing to them. They'll either get really annoyed, or (hopefully) they'll start singing along. Then you're halfway there!

- And finally, offer them incentives, such as fame, excitement, and a lifetime supply of bubble gum.

When you've got them together, throw a concert, invite your friends, and enjoy the sweet sounds of rocking has-beens!

CREATIVITY IN ACTION
Build an Amusement-Park Ride!

One of the craziest things we did this summer was build a roller coaster! We wanted a coaster that was big, fast, exciting, and like nothing we'd ever ridden before.

But that was *our* idea. What's yours? Use the next page to design your ultimate amusement-park ride. One that you would love to take a spin—or a dip, or a turn, or a loop-de-loop—on, again and again!

BRING IT ON!

How to Win at Thumb Wrestling!

Since this book is a guide to life, it's essential that we show you what to do when you get in a sticky situation. For example, Buford once challenged us to a very serious competition in the ancient sport of kings: thumb wrestling! If that happened to you, would you be prepared?

Well, now you will be, with our soon-to-be-patented process.

1. Keep your thumb high and back.

2. Keep moving. Fancy footwork—or thumb-work— is essential.

3. When backed into a corner, shout, "Hey, look out for that clown," and run.

RANDOM IDEA
The Perfect Beach Day

When we created a backyard beach, we made sure to have everything we could think of to facilitate the perfect beach day. A hot sun. Cool tunes. Rockin' waves. Awesome friends.

How would you put together your own perfect beach day?

Who would you invite? ....

What would you wear? ....

What would you bring to eat? ....

Choose one:

Water skis or a boogie board? ....

Big waves or gentle surf? ....

Building a sand castle or burying someone in the sand?

....

What else would you do to make the most of your beach day?

....

....

....

....

....

....

....

....

....

....

BUFORD'S AWESOME GUIDE TO CLEANING YOUR ROOM ... IF YOU HAVE TO

Hey, you! Yeah, you! You know how sometimes your mom gets all worked up about what a mess your room is, using words like "garbage dump" and "pigsty" and "abomination." At that point, I figure it's just easier to clean than it is to argue. But there's a way to make the cleaning faster, easier, and less work—what I like to call **THE OFFICIAL BUFORD WAY**. Read and learn.

What You Can't See Can't Hurt You

If your mom can't see it, it ain't there. Shove everything you can into your closet. When that gets full, you gotta whole 'nother storage area under your bed . . . or as I call it, closet number two.

It's All Relative

Your room only looks messy compared to other rooms in the house. So you can make it look better by messing up the other rooms! Dump some of your junk in your brother's or sister's room. Knock over a few lamps and put the vacuum cleaner in reverse. Your room will look better in no time.

Helping Hands

Even with all my awesome advice, cleaning up is still hard work. So here's my best rule of all: make someone else do it for you.

How to Escape from an Evil Reform School

After we made our mom's car fly—and it accidentally crushed our house—we were sent to a reform school so we could learn not to do dangerous things. Unfortunately, the school was evil and run like a prison. Our sister, Candace, and her friend Jeremy were kind enough to break us out, but if you ever find yourself in this situation, here are some pointers to aid in your great escape!

- Find an air vent. Despite guards, dogs, and high-tech security, every reform school has a complex series of air vents that will take you wherever you want to go.

- When in doubt, dig. A spoon is worth its weight in gold! Start a small escape tunnel and smuggle the dirt out in your pockets . . . or swallow it if you have to.

- Use bribes! Kids in reform school are deprived of all the good things in life. Enlist their help by offering them any of the following: candy bars, pens, toothpicks, lint, fresh air.

- Tie sheets together to make a rope ladder. Scale down the walls to freedom, but be sure to take time to see how high you can swing on the ladder! Escaping should be fun, right?

◊◊◊◊ **TELL YOUR OWN STORY!** ◊◊◊◊

You've heard a few of our stories. Now let's get your creative juices flowing with something we like to call "Tell Your Own Story." Using these pictures from one of our adventures, write your own text to tell a new story!

....

....

....

....

....

....

....

....

....

....

....

FILL-IN-THE-BLANKS ADVENTURE
Candace Busts the Boys!

Life doesn't always give you all the answers, and neither will we. You need to be able to find your own solutions and fill in life's blanks yourself.

So go ahead! Fill in the blanks below with crazy words to create an exciting adventure for us!

Phineas and Ferb were sitting under their ....in
                                                        NOUN
the backyard one day. Then Phineas had an idea. "Ferb, I know what

we're going to .... today!" he said. The boys started
                        VERB
building a ...., and a very .... one
                NOUN   **ADJECTIVE**
at that.

Candace, staring .... at the boys from her
                          ADVERB
window, exclaimed, "............................., it's busting time!"
                            EXCLAMATION
Quickly, she ran down the .... to tell her mom.
                                    NOUN

In the backyard, Ferb was putting the finishing touches on their

.... new project when Phineas looked around and
        ADJECTIVE
said, "Hey, where's .... ?"
                            NAME

The boys' pet .... was on a mission to fight his
                          ANIMAL

nemesis, Dr. Doofenshmirtz. The .... doctor had
                                        ADJECTIVE

created a .... -inator to take over the Tri-State Area.
              NOUN

The animal agent leaped at Dr. Doofenshmirtz and they began to

.... !
      VERB

"Look at me!" Phineas called out as he and Ferb enjoyed their

invention with their friends Buford, Baljeet, and ....
                                                          NAME

"I feel .... !" Baljeet cried.
          ADJECTIVE

But Candace was .... and ready to bust her
                          ADJECTIVE

brothers. She .... dragged her mother into the
                  ADVERB

backyard. Unfortunately, just as Mrs. Flynn-Fletcher was about to

see the boys' .... project, Dr. Doofenshmirtz's
                  ADJECTIVE

-inator accidentally fired and— .... ! Everything the
                                          SOUND EFFECT

boys had made disappeared.

"But, but, but," Candace said, ...
                                        -ING VERB

"It's okay, honey," her mom said. "You just wanted to show me

how much fun your brothers were having. Now, who wants a snack?

How about some .... ?"
                    TYPE OF FOOD (PLURAL)

CREATIVITY IN ACTION
Monster Truckin'!

If you want our advice, here it is. Whatever it takes, whatever you have to do, at some point in your life, you must take a ride in a monster truck. It's awesome! We built one for Candace this summer, and she loved it!

SHE'S A TIRE-SPINNING, GEAR-GRINDING, CLUTCH-BURNING, BACKFIRING, PAINT-TRADING, RED-LINING, OVER-HEATED, THROTTLE-STOMPING, TRUCK-DRIVING GIRL!

If you could design your own nitro-burnin', load-haulin', four-on-the-floor monster vehicle, what would it look like? Use the next page to draw the roughest, toughest monster truck you can imagine!

Top Ten Hiding Places

Sometimes it's necessary to hide.

Whatever your reason, we now give you our top ten hiding places!

10. Under the bed—a classic!

9. In the closet—but be sure to get *behind* the clothes.

8. In a cup. (You will have to shrink down for this one, so bring a shrinking device.)

7. Behind the drapes.

6. Behind Buford.

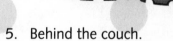

5. Behind the couch.

4. In the shower—no one looks in the shower.

3. In an alternate dimension. Tricky!

2. Under a pile of dirty clothes—no one wants to touch them.

1. In plain sight. (You won't believe how often this works!)

RANDOM IDEA
Be an Artistic Genius

It's one thing to know how to survive an arctic avalanche or how to defeat a wild mongoose in battle, but it's another thing altogether to be able to create an object of beauty.

We usually like to work with a large canvas—such as an entire continent. But remember, it's not quantity, it's quality that matters in the artistic world. Most importantly, art is what YOU think it should be, not what other people tell you it should be. So do it your way and don't listen to anyone else . . . including us!

Use the next page to create your own work of art, something you would be proud to hang in an art gallery, a great museum . . . or your room!

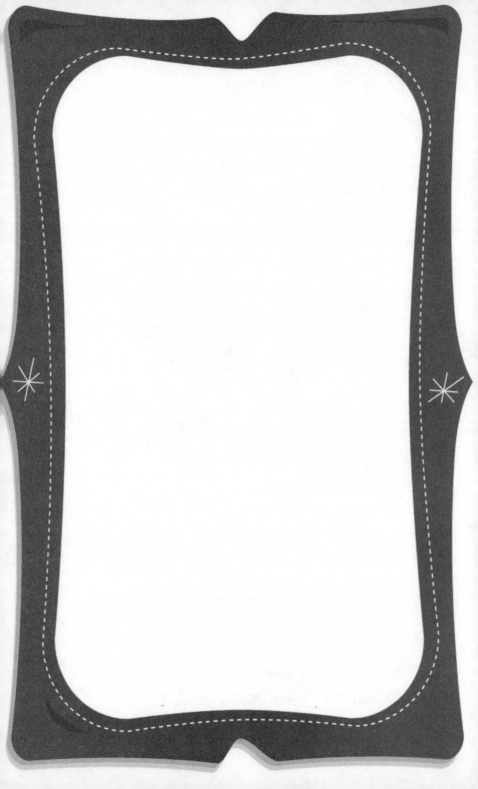

QUIZ TIME
Who Are You Most Like?

You've heard some of our advice now and are probably deciding which things to do and which not to do. That's normal. You may find you gravitate toward Ferb's view of the planet more than, say, Perry's. Well, let's find out. Which of us are you most like?

1. What's your favorite thing to wear?

A) A striped shirt

B) High-waisted pants

C) A graphic tee

D) Nothing

2. On a bright, clear, summer day, you'd most like to:

A) Plan an awesome day.

B) Build the world's largest ride.

C) Give a nerd a wedgie.

D) Disappear for a while.

3. Who would you most like to spend time with?

A) Ferb

B) Phineas

C) Baljeet—NOT!

D) Myself

4. What shape is your head?

A) Triangle

B) Rectangle

C) Square

D) Well, there's not much separation between my head and my body. But I have a bill!

SCORING (No peeking!)

Okay, give yourself one point for each time you answered A, two points for each B, three points for each C, and four points for each D. Then total up your score.

If you scored:

4-6: Congrats! You and Phineas have a lot in common.

7-9: Hey, Ferb, I know who *you're* a lot like today!

10-12: Believe it or not, you and Buford aren't all that different.

13-16: Well, you don't speak much, but neither does Perry!

HOW TO...
Invent a Secret Handshake!

A secret handshake is vital in today's topsy-turvy world. It can help you tell your friends from your frenemies . . . and it's fun! Combine the following actions in any order you like. Then write down the sequence and pass it to your friends. Do you do a Shake-Hi-Low-Hip-Bump? Or a Hip-Hip-Bump-Low-Bump?

Shake

High

Low

Bump

Hip

My secret handshake:

....!

SHAKE is a basic handshake.

HIGH is a high five.

LOW is a low five.

BUMP is a fist bump.

HIP is a hip bump.

KNOCK-KNOCK!

Tip: take time to laugh. A day without laughter is, like, really boring.

What's smarter than a talking dog?

A spelling bee!

What do you call a platypus at the North Pole? Lost!

What did Phineas say when he saw his mom's broken lamp?

Ferb, I know what we're gonna *glue* today!

Why are ghosts bad at telling fibs?

You can see right through them!

Which side of a platypus has the most fur?

The outside!

What do you call a witch who lives on the beach?

A *sand*-witch!

FINISH YOUR OWN COMIC!

WELL, FERB, OUR INTERDIMENSIONAL OUTER SPACE TEMPORAL TRANSPORTER IS NOW OPERATIONAL!

WHO KNOWS WHAT STRANGE NEW WORLDS WE MIGHT DISCOVER?!

SO, CAN YOU SEE ANYTHING?

Baljeet's Take

HOW TO SURVIVE SUMMER SCHOOL

As you all know, summer school is a chance to enjoy the fun and academic challenges of school during the three horrible months when regular school is closed. It's not nearly as all-consuming as the normal school year, but with a little preparation and thought, it can still be hard work. So here are my suggestions on how to make the most of summer school.

- Take as many classes as they will let you. Petition the principal, dean, and even the school janitor to let you take more. A lesson missed is a lesson wasted!

- The summer session is *way* too short and the teachers don't give nearly enough homework, so take on all the extra-credit projects you can.

- They won't let you stay in school all day, so when you have to go out and play, take a textbook or study guide along for fun.

- Find a study buddy! Even when school is closed, you can stay up late into the night quizzing each other and making up your own multiple-choice tests!

- Record your lessons on a tape, CD, or iPod, then play them back under your pillow so you can listen to them while you sleep. Hey, no sense in letting those eight hours go to waste.

That should help. And, of course, keep reminding yourself: September and the start of full-time school are just around the corner!

What to Do If You Lose Your Pet

Hopefully you'll never experience how bad you can feel when your pet runs away or gets lost. Our pet platypus, Perry, likes to spend time on his own and often disappears for a while every day. But when we woke up one morning and he was GONE, we did everything we could to find him. And we learned a few things that we'd like to pass on to you . . . just in case you ever need them.

- For basic dogs and cats, put up signs in your neighborhood, check with neighbors, and visit the pound in case the animal got picked up.

- If you had a larger animal, like an elephant or a blue whale, try looking around again. Seriously, those guys are pretty big. It's not like they can really hide.

- If you're looking for a tarantula . . . How cool is that?! Can we help? Those hairy little guys are awesome!

- Eagles, hawks, and other birds of prey like to go up high, so check on top of towers, steeples, and basketball players.

- Rhinoceroses love popcorn, so if you're missing one, check out your local multiplex. He's probably there.

- Armadillos can often be found in the bathroom. Don't ask us why, but we've discovered three of them taking scented bubble baths. Weird, huh?

CREATIVITY IN ACTION
Build Your Own Tree House!

Who doesn't love a tree house? And the really fun part is designing one that's just for you—one that has everything you could possibly need . . . or just plain want! Take a look at what we built and then design your own on the next page. Here are a few options you may (or may not) want to include:

Rope ladder	Flat-screen TV
Slide pole	Disco ball
Secret entrance	Guy in a monkey suit
Water-balloon catapult	Convertible roof
Official flag	Waterslide
Porthole	Alarm system
Bay window	Assorted wigs
Fridge	Zebra

USE YOUR HEAT VISION TO MAKE YOUR BROTHER'S OR SISTER'S FOOD SUPERHOT, THEN USE ICE BREATH TO MAKE IT SUPERCOLD, THEN HOT, THEN COLD AGAIN. IT'S HILARIOUS. WELL, TO ME, ANYWAY.

RANDOM IDEA
What to Do with Superpowers

Everyone wishes they had awesome superpowers—you included! But what would you do if you got them? When Ferb and I found ourselves with powers, we became a superhero called "The Beak" to fight off a menacing villain. While we don't advocate fighting, here are some things we *do* advise for you with powers beyond those of mortal men.

1) If you have superhuman strength:
Help old ladies cross the street and get cats down from trees. Actually, uh, you should be doing those things already.

2) If you have the ability to move at lightning speed:
When your parents say they're going to run to the store, actually RUN to the store and see if you can get there first.

3) If you can fly:
And if your friends like the noise of exploding fireworks (who doesn't?), fly around your yard at the speed of sound to create sonic booms!

4) If you have telescopic X-ray vision:
Use it to read comic books at the store . . . while you're still at home in bed.

5) Go ahead and save the world. (You gotta do it at least once. It's fun!)

Guide to Insta-Memory

A keen memory is vital in every aspect of life. And the best way to improve your memory is to use it! Look at this picture from one of our exciting adventures. Study it for sixty seconds, then turn the page and see how many questions you can answer about it.

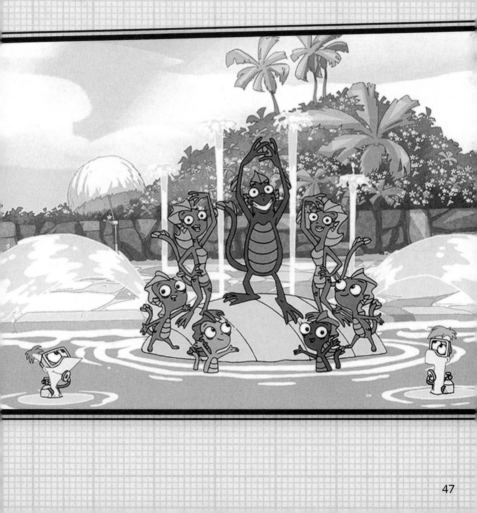

Now let's see what you can remember!

1) How many aquatic creatures did you see?

2) What side of the picture is Phineas on?

3) What is Ferb wearing?

4) Do all the aquatic creatures have tails?

5) What can you see behind the creatures, in the background of the scene?

6) Are any of the creatures carnivorous?

7) How many eyes are in the picture?

8) Was the picture a square or a rectangle?

ANSWERS

1) Seven 2) The left 3) Scuba gear . . . and probably a swimsuit! 4) Yes. Yes, they do.
5) A wall, plants, trees, a pool umbrella, and the sky. 6) Hopefully not! 7) Eighteen!
8) It's rectangular, sort of like Ferb's head.

If you got:

7-8 answers right: You have a mind like a steel trap! (That's a good thing.)
5-6 answers right: You have a great memory.
3-4 answers right: You're on your way to memory magic.
1-2 answers right: Great try! You still did better than Buford!

FERBISM: AN ANTHOLOGY OF REMARKABLE SAYINGS

It's not how much you say, it's what you say that makes an impression on others. Ferb is a master at this, and now you can be, too! Just study some of his clever comments.

Ferb on Work:

I RECKON HERDING CATTLE AIN'T FOR CITY FOLK.

Ferb on Mummification:

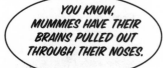

YOU KNOW, MUMMIES HAVE THEIR BRAINS PULLED OUT THROUGH THEIR NOSES.

Ferb on Sea Life:

SHARKS HAVE TO CONTINUE TO MOVE FORWARD OR THEY'LL DROWN.

Ferb on Happiness:

FUN NEVER FALLS TOO FAR FROM THE TREE HOUSE.

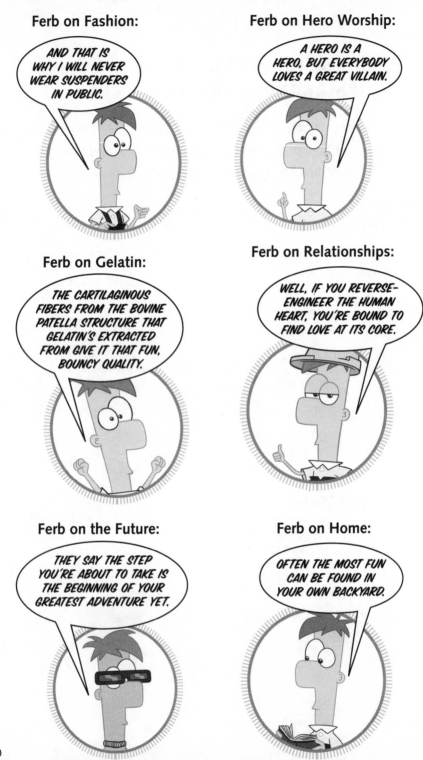

WHAT WOULD YOU DO?
Where Would You Go in Space?

Tip: see the world . . . and beyond!

It's important to get out and explore your surroundings, and the one thing surrounding all of us is outer space! We've traveled there before to help our friend Meap and to rescue Candace. If you had your own rocket . . . where would you go in space? Describe the planet you'd go to and the creatures you'd meet. Would it be negative-sixty-seven degrees? Would the aliens be friendly? Is there a place to get a Slushee Dawg?

LIFE ADVICE
Set a Record!

Nothing beats setting a new world record. We once set three in one day with a giant bowling ball and a little imagination. For us, it's not about competing or beating anyone else but having fun setting our own personal records! What are your great accomplishments? Can you beat your own records?

Furthest-Thrown
Paper Airplane: .... (feet)

Most Jumps,
Jumping on
One Foot: ....

Most Books
Balanced on
Head: ....

Fastest Time
Singing our
Phineas and Ferb
Theme Song: .... (seconds)

Tallest Stack
of Things: .... (feet)

Farthest
Jump: .... (feet)

Longest Nonstop
Book-Reading
Session: .... (hours)

Deepest Pile of
Dirty Clothes
.... (inches)

Longest Word
You Know: .... (letters)

Most Pancakes
Eaten in One
Sitting: ....

BUFORD'S TAKE

BE MANNERFUL!
Buford Tells It Like It Is

Okay, once again it's up to me to tell you guys how to live your lives. So here's my two cents on bein' polite and obeying mannerishness.

- When you meet someone in the street, say, "Hey." Unless it's somebody important, like the queen. Then you say, "Howdy-do?" Unless it's your teacher and you didn't turn in your homework. Then just run.

- If you sneeze, say, "Gesundheit." No, wait, that's if someone else sneezes. Say, "Excuse me." Actually, no, wait, first you're supposed to cover your mouth and then . . . Okay, let's make this easy. Don't sneeze.

- When you get a gift, send thank-you notes right away. . . . No more than a year or two later for sure. That's for gifts. I'm not sure what kind of note to send when you just take something from somebody without asking first, but it never hurts to be polite.

- When at a hoity-toity restaurant (that's French for "fancy"), always use the outside fork to eat your salad. They look at you funny when you use the knife.

- Always hold a door open for a lady. You can do the same for some guy if he's holding a lot of packages, or carrying a dog in a purse, or whatever. You can also hold a door open for a nerd, but then shut it right when he tries to go through. It's not genius, but it's good for a laugh.

CREATIVITY IN ACTION
Build Your Own Pirate Ship!

Ahoy, matey! Aye, 'tis true, when we voyaged in search of Badbeard's lost treasure, we built our own stout pirate ship from the mizzenmast to the poop deck. Now, ye landlubber, 'tis your turn to craft a seaworthy vessel . . . or walk the plank!

Translation: draw your own pirate ship on the next page!

HOW TO . . .
Control the Weather

Let's face it. Sometimes singing "Rain, rain, go away, come again some other day" just doesn't cut it. If you're in the mood for sunbathing or are craving some snowboarding action on a half-pipe, you can't just wait for the weather to change. Therefore, we now offer you our fail-safe tips for mastering Mother Nature!

Rain

For small areas, such as your backyard or bedroom, point your garden hose straight toward the sky and crank it up. For larger areas, there's always the traditional rain dance.

Snow

Grab your sled and put on your mittens, it's time for winter! We used a snow-cone machine and some air-conditioning units set on high. If it worked for us, it should work for you!

Sandstorm

Now why would you want to do that?

Sun

Technically, the sun is always out, so if clouds are blocking your rays, just get above the clouds. We suggest a hot-air balloon, biplane, or really tall stilts.

Buford Van Stomm Presents

WOULD YOU RATHER?

Sometimes in life you gotta make choices.
Like now. Pick one:

Would you rather I give you a wedgie or make you eat a bug?
(Hint: go for the bug.)

FILL-IN-THE-BLANKS ADVENTURE
Phineas and Ferb's Alaskan Jaunt

In this exciting adventure, fill in the blanks with crazy words to make a zany Phineas and Ferb story!

"...................................! I never thought we'd be ....
      EXCLAMATION   ANIMAL

-sledding across Alaska," Phineas said.

"And I never thought I'd be so cold and ....,"
                                        ADJECTIVE

Candace complained.

"Hey, where's Perry?" Phineas asked.

Perry the Platypus had transformed into Agent P and was far

across the ice trying to .... Dr. Doofenshmirtz, but
                                 VERB

the .... doctor was ready and waiting. He trapped
          ADJECTIVE

Perry in a .... and explained his plan to collect all the
               NOUN

ice in .... and use it to take over the Tri-State Area!
        PLACE

Meanwhile, Phineas and Ferb's sled came to a ....
                                       ADJECTIVE

stop. Blocking their path was a giant, ... snow-
                            ADJECTIVE

.... and it was angry!
NOUN

"It's going to .... us!" Candace screamed.
VERB

But Ferb cracked his .... and the sled leaped forward.
NOUN

The giant snow thing raced .... after them and the
ADVERB

chase was on.

But within ...., Agent P broke free and kicked
AMOUNT OF TIME

Dr. Doofenshmirtz in the .... Dr. Doofenshmirtz's
BODY PART

mammoth block of stolen ice slipped away and slid right between

the boys and their .... pursuer. They were saved!
ADJECTIVE

"Well," Ferb said, "I guess that's about all the ....
NOUN

the human heart can take for ....day/s."
NUMBER

LIFE ADVICE
How to Speak English in England

WHEN WE TRAVELED TO ENGLAND TO VISIT OUR GRANDPARENTS, I WAS SURPRISED TO FIND OUT HOW MANY DIFFERENCES THERE WERE BETWEEN AMERICAN ENGLISH AND ENGLISH ENGLISH.

HE'S SPOT ON.

SO WE THOUGHT IT MIGHT BE HELPFUL TO SHOW YOU SOME OF THE DIFFERENCES IN CASE YOU DECIDE TO VISIT.

Instead of "TV," the British say "telly."

LOOK! I'M ON A TELLY!

Pants. You really must be careful with this one. In England "pants" means your underwear!

A "bobby" isn't just another guy. It's a word for "policeman"!

A BOBBY? WHAT? WHERE?!?

You would say everything is "hunky-dory" if things are going well. Got it? Great. Grand. Dandy!

And an "eggplant" is a person who enjoys knitting with cavemen. (No, we made that last one up.)

CHEERIO!

What right do Phineas and Ferb have to publish a book of life lessons? What do they know? I'm older than they are! I have more life experience. If anyone should be writing a "guide to life," it's me! In fact, I think I will. From this point on, I'm in charge.

Oh, right. When Mom puts me in charge, I am rarely *totally* in charge. It comes in degrees. That's the first thing I'll show you in MY guide to life: ***How to Tell How Much You Are in Charge***, by Candace Flynn.

Conditionally In Charge

This means you're in charge on the condition that something actually happens . . . like . . . if aliens land in the yard, moose stampede through the house, or the next ice age begins. Then you're in charge.

Probationally In Charge

Okay, this means that you have certain limited powers and responsibilities for a specified time, like, say, a day, while your parents watch to see if you mess up. Which *I* never would.

DEFINE "IN CHARGE."

Ambidextrously In Charge

This means you're in charge not just with your right hand or your left hand, but with both hands equally and . . . Wait . . . that makes no sense. This is ridiculous.

From this point on, I am conclusively, absolutely, and totally in charge! Well, for the next three pages, at least!

CANDACE ON SHOPPING
How to Navigate the Mall

1) The normal way:

Show up early, before the crowds, and leave at a reasonable hour.

 **The Candace way:**

No one who is anyone shows up before noon. The Candace shopper is always fashionably late. And the salesperson should have to force you out when it's time to close.

2) The normal way:

If you want to save money, look for the sales rack, holiday sales, and off-season items.

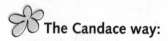 **The Candace way:**

Sale items are so five minutes ago. You must dress to impress. I go for what's new and what's trendy, but I don't overlook the classics (such as a red shirt and white skirt), which never go out of style.

3) The normal way:

Start at one end of the mall and methodically work your way to the other end.

The Candace way:

Snag a mall map and plot your shopping path so that you pass the Slushee Dawg (where Jeremy works) at least five times. Okay, maybe six.

CANDACE KNOWS BEST
How to Win Family-Picnic Contests

I'm a little competitive. Okay, I'm a *lot* competitive. So when it comes to a contest, I'm in it to win it. If you want a family-picnic trophy in your future, listen up. This is the gold.

1) Practice, practice, practice.

And then practice some more. Don't get distracted by any siblings who might be building a superpowered suit or digging a tunnel to the center of the Earth.

2) Keep your eyes on the prize.

Not *literally* on the prize. If you spend the whole time staring at the blue ribbon, you'll trip over your own feet. What I mean is: focus on what you're doing. *Sheesh!*

3) Teamwork! Teamwork! Teamwork!

Unless you're doing it on your own—then it's every woman for herself!

MY 411

How to Bust Your Brothers

Stop what you're doing and get a pencil and paper. This may be the most important advice you get in your entire life. I am about to give you the crucial 411 on how to bust your brothers.

1) Be prepared.

This is essential. Start by stretching. Skipping this often-overlooked step can leave you vulnerable to pulled muscles. Prepare yourself mentally by focusing on your goal. Say to yourself, "I will bust the boys. I will bust the boys." Say it until you mean it. Do you have running shoes on? You'd better! Got Mom on your phone's speed dial? Good. It's busting time.

2) Get evidence.

No one is going to believe your rantings and ravings about all the things your brothers do. You need cold, hard evidence. Photos. Audio recordings. Video. Physical evidence is best. Eyewitnesses are unreliable, so unless you've got the mayor swearing on a stack of mayor books, I wouldn't bother.

3) Show your mom.

This seems simple enough, but it is the step that so often goes awry. If you figure out how to accomplish this one, please let me know.

Now, if you'll excuse me, I'm going to take a copy of this incriminating *Guide to Life* and show it to my mom. My brothers are going **down, down, down**!

Baljeet's Take

GUIDE TO FEELING SUPERIOR WITH BALJEET!

It is uncommonly fun to look up new words in the dictionary—words that no one else knows—and then use them around adults, making yourself look smarter than they are. Here are some examples of crazy *real* words you can use.

Obnubilate

This is a verb that means "to cloud over or darken."

*My mood **obnubilates** whenever Buford comes into the room.*

Jactitation

This is a noun that means "a false claim or cruel boast."

*Buford made a **jactitation** that I was scared of ladybugs, when really I'm only troubled by them.*

Maunder

This last one is a verb that means "to speak in a rambling manner."

*Ferb chooses his words carefully and is not one to **maunder**.*

Now, if you are feeling particularly impish (that means "playful" or "goofy"), make up your own words and use them *as if* they are real.

Fantabulous

This would be the combination of "fantastic" and "fabulous."

*Phineas and Ferb's underground rocket ride was **fantabulous**!*

Angriveinous

This is how a person gets when they are so mad that a vein on their neck or forehead bulges out.

*I get so **angriveinous** when Buford spouts his **jactitations** about me.*

Now you try. Make up your own wacky words.

WORD: ....

DEFINITION: ....

....

USE IT IN A SENTENCE: ....

....

• •

WORD: ....

DEFINITION: ....

....

USE IT IN A SENTENCE: ....

....

HILARIOUS HILARITY

Nothing to learn here, reader, just sit back and laugh.

Why don't any of the animals in the jungle ever want to play cards?

There are too many *cheetahs*!

What is a mummy's favorite kind of music?

Wrap music!

What do you call a skeleton who won't get out of bed?

Lazybones!

What do you say when you meet a two-headed monster?

Hello, hello!

What is The Beak's favorite sandwich?

A super*hero*!

What kind of dessert goes best with an antigravity machine?

A float!

What time is it when a platypus breaks through your wall?

Time to get a new wall!

VITAL LIFE INFO
Songwriting 101

When we found out that our mom was Lindana, the one-hit-wonder pop star, we decided to form Phineas and the Ferbtones and write our own hit song. Now it's your turn. Write new lyrics to a tune you already know, like "Jingle Bells." Here's an example:

> *Jingle bells, Candace smells, Buford cries all day.*
> *And Baljeet, he is so sweet, in an annoying way—hey!*

Now you try it. First, think of a song you know well:

....

Now change the lyrics so that they are all about you:

....

....

....

Try to have the same number of syllables in each line as the original song. Here's one about Ferb to the tune of "For He's a Jolly Good Fellow!"

> *Yes, Ferb is an interesting fellow.*
> *His favorite color is yellow.*
> *He won't say much 'cause he's mellow.*
> *He loves him a piece of pie!*

Pick another song, maybe a different style altogether:

....

Now change the lyrics so they are all about us:

....

....

....

....

Sometimes it helps to think of a rhyme and work backward. We did that with this one, sung to the tune of "Old MacDonald."

> *Candace says you're goin' down,*
> *Down, down, down, down, down.*
> *As busting queen she wears the crown,*
> *Down, down, down, down, down.*
> *With a bust, bust here and a bust, bust there,*
> *Here a bust, there a bust, everywhere she must bust.*
> *Candace says you're goin' down,*
> *Down, down, down, down, down!*

PHINEAS AND FERB TRIVIA

Observation is key in life. Have you been aware and paying attention during all of our adventures? Let's see what you can remember.

1) At what lake do Phineas and Ferb vacation?
   A. Lake Eerie
   B. Lake Nose
   C. Lake Smellslikebufordsshoes

2) Who are the members of the Ferbettes?
   A. Isabella and the Fireside Girls
   B. Mini Ferbs wearing skirts
   C. A herd of singing cows

3) What device does Phineas invent when he wonders what Perry is saying?
   A. The world's biggest catapult
   B. A Platypusionary
   C. A Perry Translator—also known as an animal translator

4) What three world records did Phineas and Ferb break in one day?
   A. World's largest bowling ball, world's largest game of pinball, and breaking two world records in one day
   B. World's fastest roller coaster, world's largest game of pinball, and world's best pet platypus
   C. World's largest bowling ball, world's largest bubble-gum bubble, and world's only freckle in the shape of George Washington (on Buford's leg)

5) What happened to the audience while watching *The Curse of the Princess Monster?*
   A. They were transformed into old people.
   B. They didn't like the movie and stormed out of the theater.
   C. All of the above

6) What kind of battle occurred between Buford and Phineas in a boxing ring?
   A. A boxing match
   B. A thumb-wrestling match
   C. A food-eating contest

7) What do Phineas and Ferb make for Isabella when she gets her tonsils out?
   A. A teddy bear that looks like Phineas—by coincidence.
   B. The biggest ice-cream sundae ever!
   C. Genetically altered roses that never lose their smell.

8) Who wins the Greek chariot race that Phineas and Ferb create?
   A. Candace
   B. Baljeet
   C. Perry

9) Phineas and Ferb make some robots in order to get more projects done. What are they called?
   A. P2D2s
   B. Phinedroids and Ferbots
   C. Phineas X and Ferb Y

10) What is the name of the book that Baljeet uses to help Phineas and Ferb find out about shoelaces?
    A. *Shoelaces for the Creative Soul*
    B. *Tying Your Shoes: You Can Do It!*
    C. *Useless Shoelace Facts, Volume 8*

ANSWERS

1) B   2) A   3) C   4) A   5) C   6) B   7) B   8) A   9) B   10) C

Okay, give yourself one point for each one you got right and total up your score.

If you scored:

1-2: Nice. You're clearly a fan!
3-5: Awesome! You've been paying attention.
6-8: Amazing! You have a keen eye for detail and a great memory!
9-10: That's incredible! You know more about us than we do.

Guide to Letter Writing

At some point in your life, you're gonna have to write a letter. Why not make it fun? That's why we invented the *Phineas and Ferb Insta-Letter!* Just choose from the multiple-choice items below to create your very own letter—instantly!

DEAR A) Friend, B) Relative, C) Complete Stranger,

HOW ARE YOU? I HOPE YOU'RE A) healthy. B) making the most of every day. C) out of jail.

THANK YOU FOR THE A) letter
B) chainsaw C) goat
YOU RECENTLY SENT ME. IT WAS JUST A) perfect for building a roller coaster, B) my size, C) awful,
AND I CAN'T THANK YOU
A) enough.
B) at all.
C) without laughing.

THINGS HERE HAVE BEEN
A) interesting. B) crazy. C) on fire.

GRANDMA BROKE HER A) lamp, B) hip, C) promise not to burp, *AND IT'S BEEN HARD ON ALL OF US . . . ESPECIALLY UNCLE JOE.*

WHO KNEW HE A) loved B) loathed C) dressed up as *GRANDMA SO MUCH? WELL, FERB DID—BUT THE REST OF US SURE DIDN'T!*

I SHOULD PROBABLY A) wrap this up, B) get out of bed, C) go shark-diving, *BECAUSE IT'S ALMOST TIME FOR* A) Candace to bring Mom out! B) my nap! C) the Revolutionary War!

IF YOU'RE EVER IN TOWN, PLEASE A) stop by to have some fun. B) enjoy a Slushee Dawg on us. C) watch your back!

    A) Seize the day,
    B) Sincerely,
    C) Good riddance,

(YOUR SIGNATURE HERE)...

⊶⊷⊷⊷⊷⊷⊷ TELL YOUR OWN STORY! ⊷⊷⊷⊷⊷⊷⊶

Take these pictures from one of our adventures and write your own text to tell a new story!

....

....

....

....

....

....

....

....

....

....

....

....

....

....

....

....

....

CREATIVITY IN ACTION
Design a Mini Golf Course

Do you remember when we created our own miniature golf course?

YES. IT WAS FUN TO PUTTER AROUND ON IT.

How would you design the ultimate course? What obstacles would you create? A windmill? A dragon? A fifty-foot Candace?

What would the theme be? Pirates? The Old West? What about a platypus theme?

Would it be easy? Or difficult? Or both?

Use the next page to design the best, the greatest, the most amazing mini golf course ever!

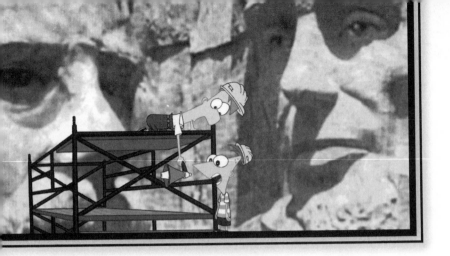

HOW TOS . . . AROUND THE WORLD

Not every one of our how-to suggestions can be done in your own backyard. Some require that you venture to exotic far-flung cities, or to one of the wonders of the world. (What can we say? We like to travel!) So without any further ado, here are our *worldly* how-tos!

1) How to clean Mount Rushmore
With a toothbrush . . . and a lot of time.

2) How to climb the Eiffel Tower
Very carefully.

3) How to reach the North Pole
By sleigh (using eight reindeer). Duh!

4) How to jump over the Grand Canyon
Sneak up on it when it's not looking.

5) How to cross—

Well, well, well, it looks like someone's writing a book.

How lucky for me, Dr. Heinz Doofenshmirtz. This is the perfect opportunity to spread my message . . . of evil!

As of this moment, right now, right this second, while you are reading this sentence, I am officially taking over this ridiculous "guide to life." Besides, I have my own valuable life lessons to share. What, you don't believe me? Fine. First, my qualifications . . .

DOOF YOU KNOW?
Facts About the Good Doctor

1) I am a proud member of the evil society Love Muffin. Although, to be honest, I am a few years behind in my dues.

2) I am the proud father of a lovely teenage girl, Vanessa. She's not evil yet, but give her time.

3) I can whistle in three (3!) languages. So there.

4) I was once married . . . and if you don't think that's an accomplishment, then you obviously have never been married.

5) I wrote this entire page by myself with very little assistance from Norm, despite what he might tell you.

Now, Dr. Doofenshmirtz says you may turn the page.

THE KEY TO SUCCESS IN LIFE
-Inators!

Learning to make an -inator is an essential skill in life. Here's a list of some of my greatest -inators so that you can avoid repeating my mistakes . . . er . . . I mean, stealing my fantastic ideas.

- Ballgown-inator *(It was more evil than it sounds.)*
- Bread-inator
- Brew-inator
- De-love-inator
- Eras-inator *(on the end of my Pencil-inator)*
- Everything-evil-inator
- Freez-inator
- Gloom-inator
- Hot-dog-revenge-inator *(Hey, they can't all be gems!)*
- Invis-inator
- Kick-inator
- Make-up-your-mind-inator
- Melt-inator
- Misbehav-inator
- Monkey-enslav-inator *(Not to be confused with the Monkey-engag-inator)*
- Monster-truck-away-inator
- Mountain-out-of-a-molehill-inator
- Music-video-clip-inator
- Poop-inator *(Yes, yes, it's just what it sounds like.)*
- Read-my-mind-inator
- Scorch-inator *(Careful. It's hot!)*
- Slow-motion-inator
- Smell-inator
- Space-laser-inator
- Ugly-inator *(Which, oddly enough, was my best looking -inator.)*
- Zinc-inator

DESIGN YOUR OWN-INATOR

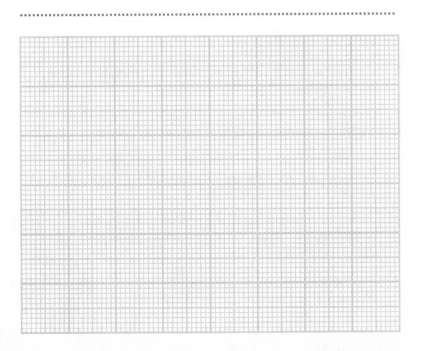

Fine! You think you can do better, Mr. Big-Shot Smarty-Pants? Well, put your pencil where your mouth is! Not literally—that's a germ-fest waiting to happen. What I mean is, let's see if you can design a better -inator than I can!

-Inator name: ....

What it does: ....

How it works: ....

Why it's better than Dr. Doofenshmirtz's -inators:

....

DR. DOOFENSHMIRTZ'S TOP TEN TIPS FOR LIFE

I hereby give you my hard-won wisdom in what I like to call "Dr. Doofenshmirtz's Top Ten Tips for Life." Oh, it already says that at the top of the page, doesn't it? Well, never mind then.

1. Don't set your sights too high. Why stress yourself out trying to take over the world when you can much more easily control the Tri-State Area?

2. Live in the moment. Nothing good comes from constantly dwelling on things from your past. Such as all those years your parents made you work as a lawn gnome, late into the night, all alone . . .

3. Always install a self-destruct button. I'm not sure why, but it's really important.

4. Make your traps platypus-proof. This may sound obvious, but believe me, it's worth double-checking. You'll thank me later.

5. Brush your teeth after every meal.

6. Buy low, sell high. I don't know what that means, but I heard it on an infomercial.

7. Live each day as if it is your last. Of course, that's much more applicable to me, seeing as how I am accident prone.

8. Take time to stop and smell the roses . . . because I have altered them with my Hyper-Pollen-Smell-inator, which will turn everyone who sniffs my flowers into unwilling slaves!

9. When you're feeling down, sing a song! Unless it's rap or hip-hop. I hate those. Or country. Or that noisy punk stuff. Or contemporary jazz.

10. Never give up. Even if you lose one hundred times out of one hundred, like me. Keep trying!

And in closing, let me just say one more thing:
Curse you, Reader the Reader-puss!

GREAT GOOGLIE-MOOGLIE!

What kind of warped individual gave four whole pages to Dr. Doofenshmirtz to spout his evil propaganda? That's madness. The animal agents of Organization Without a Cool Acronym (OWCA), including Perry the Platypus, deserve their own time. And, unless my intern Carl Karl feels the need to interrupt . . .

. . . that time is now.

NO, I'M GOOD, SIR

 OUR 411

How to Be a Secret Agent!

1) First and foremost, all agents need a code name. Here at OWCA, we've chosen to go with letters of the alphabet according to type of animal. What? You thought Agent "P" stood for "princess"?

2) It is essential that you can move quickly in the field. Lives hang in the balance. What kind of vehicle would you choose for a speedy getaway?

3) You definitely need a secret tool. Grappling hook? All-purpose lock pick? Boomeranging fedora?

4) Style counts: what kind of hat would you wear? Bowler? Beret? Beanie?

5) And most importantly, who would be your nemesis? (This can include your siblings.)

SERVE YOUR COUNTRY!
Draw Your Own Animal Agents

We're always on the lookout for new agents, and while you may be a bit too "human" to fit the bill, perhaps you can come up with some suggestions for our next key operative. Agent L (a llama)? Agent G (a gopher)? Agent R (a ring-tailed lemur)? You can think *outside* the box, but make sure you draw *inside* the box!

KNOW YOUR OPERATIVES!
Agent P Trivia

We do our best to keep information about our agents secret, so it's important to see how much has leaked out to the public. Carl, hit them with the bright lights and let's start the interrogation.

1) Where is Agent P's lair?

2) Name three ways Perry can maneuver through the air.

3) Where does Perry keep his tools?

4) What other agent/s, besides Agent P, has/have fought Dr. Doofenshmirtz?

ANSWERS

1) Under Phineas and Ferb's house 2) His hover car, his jet pack, and his parachute/ hang glider 3) In his fedora. 4) Peter the Panda, Agent W the Whale, and more!

OPERATING ROBOT PARENTS!

It is essential for secret agents to have the right tools at their disposal, and sometimes that means creating robot replicas of your family members. Carl did this with the Flynn-Fletcher family.

AND I SENT THE DAD ROBOT IN TO IMPERSONATE MR. FLETCHER FOR THE DAY.

Now what if YOU were the agent? What if YOU had a robot replica that looked and sounded exactly like one of your parents?

How would you use it? ....

What would it look like? ....

What would you have it do? ....

....

....

Excellent work! At this rate, you'll be a secret agent in no time. But before we sign off, one final lesson. And this is perhaps the most important one of all: the essentials of mustache management! First and foremost, a thorough brushing three times a day is—

I THINK WE'VE TAKEN UP ENOUGH OF THEIR TIME, SIR. GOOD-BYE, EVERYBODY!

SORRY ABOUT THAT! WE TOOK A QUICK WRITING BREAK TO TRAVEL TO THE FUTURE. BUT HAVE NO FEAR, DEAR READER, WE'RE BACK. NOW, FOR MORE LIFE ADVICE!

HOW TO . . .
Befriend an Aquatic Beast

When you encounter a large, slithering sea serpent, you may find that you want to befriend it. Well, better to befriend it than to be-*enemy* it, we say. Here are some simple ways to extend the hand of friendship to an underwater individual.

▶ Smile. Wave. Bow. Curtsy. Okay, now stop—you might freak it out.

▶ Introduce yourself: "Hi, my name is ____. I'm an air-breathing, nonaquatic humanoid. And you are . . . ?"

▶ Give it a snack. You don't want it eyeing you if it starts to get hungry.

▶ Play a game with it. Probably a water-based game is best. They're not great at board games.

▶ And remember: be kind. Monsters are people, too!

HOW TO BE A STRONG LEADER

Isabella here! As head of my Fireside Girls troop, I've had to learn a thing or two about being a strong leader. Someday *you* may need to step up and lead the way, so here are some dos and don'ts to help you when that time comes!

DELEGATE

DON'T take on everything by yourself.

DO delegate, giving some of your work to others and trusting them to get it done.

DON'T boss other people around.

DO present clear, consistent instructions to your men . . . um, girls . . . um, troop. Can I start over?

DON'T BOSS

STAY FOCUSED

DON'T change your focus willy-nilly.

DO keep your priorities straight:
1) Fireside Girls 2) Phineas 3) everything else.

DON'T give up.

DO go for it. If you stop trying,
how will you ever get your
Underwater Go-Kart patch,
Outer Space Crocheting patch,
or Appalachian Monkey–
Rescuing patch?

DON'T GIVE UP

Figure A

CREATIVITY IN ACTION
Invent a New Sport

You know how to do this activity by now, don't you?

We made up a cool new sport. (See Figure A, above.)
Now YOU make up a cool new sport. (See Figure B, next
page.) Easy as pie! Go for it!

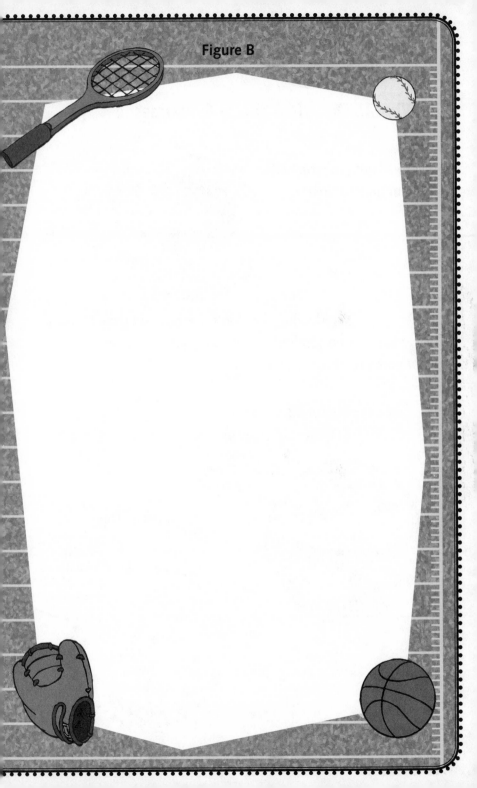

What to Do When You're Embarrassed

We all get embarrassed from time to time.

OR ALL THE TIME.

It's part of life. But that doesn't mean you have to like it. Here are some surefire ways to cope when you feel a wave of embarrassment coming on.

Act like you did it on purpose.

I MEANT TO DUMP SPAGHETTI ON MY SHIRT

Deny. Deny. Deny.

I'M NOT BLUSHING. MY CHEEKS ARE SUNBURNED.

Hide.

Point at someone else and run.

QUIZ TIME
What's My Amazing Circus Talent?

One of our best days this summer was the day we built an entire circus in our own backyard. We loved seeing the surprising—and amazing—circus talents our friends had! Unfortunately, we can't advise you on your circus potential until you tell us a little more about yourself. Answer the questions below to find out if you're better suited to walk the high wire, swing from the trapeze, dress up as a crazy clown, or put your head in a lion's mouth!

1) Which of the following are you most skilled at?

A) Walking a straight line
B) Swinging on a swing set
C) Getting hit with a pie
D) Putting your head into things

2) How do you prefer to travel?

A) By unicycle
B) By trapeze
C) In a tiny car with ten other passengers
D) In a lion's stomach

3) People often describe me as:

A) Well-balanced.

B) Flighty.

C) Always clowning around.

D) Delicious.

4) The best circus name for me would be:

A) High-Walking Wally.

B) The Flying Fandango.

C) Boppo.

D) The late, great Alfonso.

SCORING

Give yourself one point for each time you answered A, two points for each B, three for each C, and four for each D. Then total up your score.

If you scored:

4-6: You'll be a tightrope-walker extraordinaire!
7-9: Prepare for a swinging life on the trapeze.
10-13: Get out your big floppy shoes, you clown!
14-16: Uh-oh. I hope you have life insurance, Mr. or Ms. Lion Tamer!

Stay Informed

Your life will be richer and more rewarding if you stay informed. Sometimes reading the *Danville Daily* gives us cool ideas about what to do that day!

GORILLA WORLD'S STRONGEST ANIMAL

By Gordon Grey, Staff Writer

TANZANIA—Scientists have proven that the lowland gorilla is the strongest animal in the world. No human could possibly survive a battle with an angry gorilla—not even with some sort of steel exoskeleton enhancing the person's powers. I'd sure like to see someone try, but it just seems impossible.

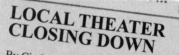

FERB, I KNOW WHAT WE'RE GOING TO DO TODAY!

LOCAL THEATER CLOSING DOWN

By Cindy Valencia, Staff Writer

DANVILLE—The Danville city council confirmed today that the beloved Danville Center Theater will be closing its doors for good at the end of the week due to lack of funds. Theater managers said it would take a miracle to keep the theater alive now. For example, if someone put on a huge show—the biggest Danville had ever seen—to raise money and awareness, *that* might save it.

FERB, I KNOW WHAT ELSE WE'RE GOING TO DO TODAY!

If you were a writer for the *Danville Daily*, what article would you write? Can you write one that might give us our next great idea?

HOW TO . . .
Survive a Shipwreck

Top ten tips for surviving on a desert island, from the kids who did it in style!

1. **Shelter.** This is your first priority. It doesn't have to be fancy or anything. A modest three-bedroom, two-bath place is fine.

2. **Water.** Make sure it's fresh. And preferably not the bubbly kind—it tickles Ferb's nose.

3. **Food.** It's best to have fruits and vegetables . . . with fast food only occasionally.

4. **Clothes.** The best three looks we've found are Safari Gear, Jungle Boy, and Castaway Chic.

5. **Fire.** This is great for warmth and cooking. To start one, you can use two sticks, a piece of flint, or our favorite: a solar-thermal-condenser unit.

6. **Signal for Help.** Fire (see #5) is great for this, but you can also get attention with a giant S.O.S. made out of rocks, smoke signals, or a huge Broadway-style sign with lights.

7. **Wildlife.** Dealing with the native creatures is essential. If they get too smelly, be sure to give the monkeys a shower.

8. **Music.** Okay, this one is not essential, but it makes everything better.

9. **Sand.** It's your friend! You'll undoubtedly have a LOT of sand, so make use of it. You can build sand castles, sand figures, and *sand*-wiches.

10. **Boat.** It's fun playing castaway, but when you're ready to leave you'll need a boat. Or a helicopter—but that's harder to make with coconuts and palm fronds.

DEALING WITH UNREASONABLE FEARS

Okay, first off, I do not know why Phineas and Ferb have asked me to cover this subject. I am not a particularly fearful person. However, I am familiar with many of the common phobias that would be considered by some people to be unreasonable, so I will continue.

Fear of Vengeful Pirate Skeletons

Although very scary, I admit, the chances of running into any vengeful pirate skeletons, especially on dry land, are exceedingly small. So do not be such a worrywart.

Fear of Wedgies

Okay, now this is not an unreasonable fear at all. In fact, my heightened awareness to potential wedgie threats has protected me many a Tuesday afternoon, when science club lets out. Stay strong, my friends.

Fear of Being Taken to an Island Where a Mad Scientist is Combining Men with Animals in Horrifying Experiments That Quickly Spiral Out of His Control!

I saw this one on television. Very creepy. My advice: do not go there.

Fear of Cauliflower

Okay, it is true that cauliflower will not hurt you—and is actually good for you. Therefore, this could be considered an unreasonable fear by some. But I am scared of cauliflower. So what? Who are you to judge me?

Fear of Portals to Other Worlds, Gigantic Roller Coasters, and Time-Travel Machines

Actually, in Danville, this is a pretty realistic fear. You're on your own with this one.

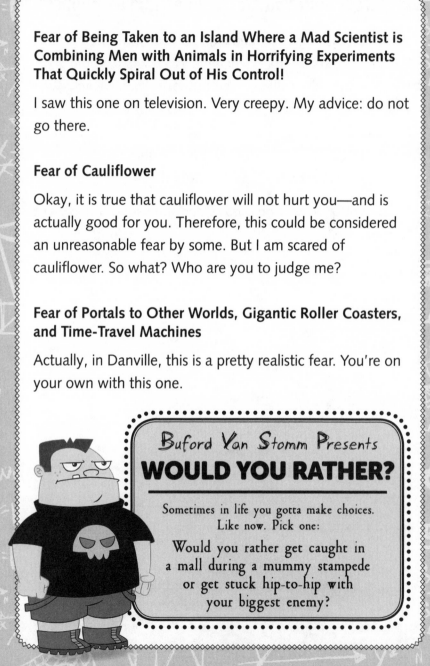

Buford Van Stomm Presents
WOULD YOU RATHER?

Sometimes in life you gotta make choices.
Like now. Pick one:

Would you rather get caught in a mall during a mummy stampede or get stuck hip-to-hip with your biggest enemy?

WHAT WOULD YOU DO?
WHEN Would You Go . . . in a Time Machine?

It's important to get out and explore your surroundings. We told you that before, when we asked where you'd go in space. But why limit yourself to space when we've got a whole other dimension (time!) to mess around with?! If you had a time machine, like the one at the Danville Museum, you could go anywhere in time. But the question isn't where you would go. . . . WHEN would you go?

Describe the era you'd go to and the people you'd want to meet.

....

....

....

....

....

....

....

....

....

....

....

....

....

....

....

....

....

....

LIFE ADVICE
Meet New People!

Old friends are the best friends, it's true. But it's also important to meet new people and expand your social circle. That's why we built the Mix 'n' Mingler—to help us meet lots of new people quickly. If you could meet someone new today, what kind of person would you most like them to be? Pick one word from each column to see who you might meet.

Column A	Column B	Column C
Mad scientist	Denmark	Sings opera
Scorpion wrangler	Tahiti	Draws cartoons
Goofy dentist	The North Pole	Does cartwheels
Rock star	Mars	Trips old people
Newborn baby	The Gobi desert	Wears a tutu
Candy-maker	Las Vegas	Kisses frogs
Whistling plumber	Tokyo	Cries for no reason
Cheek-pinching grandma	The Australian outback	Burps constantly

Write in your new acquaintances here:

A...
    from ....
     who ....

A...
    from ....
     who ....

A...
    from ....
     who ....

A...
    from ....
     who ....

A...
    from ....
     who ....

HAUNTING YOUR HOUSE

Halloween is a great excuse to dress up in a spooky outfit and eat lots of gummy worms, but you don't have to wait for October 31st to create a truly original haunted house. Here are some tips to *scarify* your abode any day of the year!

DO use old sheets to make ghosts.

DON'T invite real ghosts. They're fun, but impossible to get rid of after the party.

• •

DO stuff old clothes to make dummies.

DON'T stuff clothes while people are still in them.

• •

DO play creepy music.

DON'T play Lindana's music, even if your sister SAYS it's creepy.

• •

DO ask your parents' permission to use their stuff.

DON'T ask permission AFTER you've already ripped your dad's best suit to make a zombie costume.

DO put on scary makeup.

DON'T put on your mom's makeup.

DO dress up like Frankenstein's monster, a vampire, or a zombie.

DON'T dress up like a pumpkin, a superhero, or a princess. When was the last time you saw a spooky princess?

DO set up creepy areas like a graveyard, a castle, or a mad scientist's lair.

DON'T use themes such as a Laundromat, a sports game, or the Fourth of July.

FINISH YOUR OWN COMIC!

WE'VE BEEN HIT!

AAAAAAAH!

Animal Translating

Do you ever wonder what your pet is really saying to you? Well now, thanks to our revolutionary Animal Translator, you can finally know what Fido and Mr. Snootikins are trying to tell you!

DOG:

WOOF = I'm hungry.

BARK = I'm hungry.

GRRR = Get away. I'm hungry.

CAT:

MEOW = Whatever

MEOWWWW = Who cares?

MROWR = Yawn

BIRD:

CHIRP = Hello

RODENT:

SQUEAK = I say, could I trouble you to clean out my cage? Much thanks in advance. Good day to you.

What does your pet say to you? ....

....

113

FIRESIDE GIRLS NATURE TIPS

FIRESIDE GIRLS HANDBOOK

Hey, guys! As Fireside Girls, we have a lot of experience in the great outdoors. And if we want to earn our Sharing Nature-Tips-with-Others patch, we need to pass our knowledge on to you!

MOSS GROWS ON THE NORTH SIDE OF TREES. AND THE SOUTH, EAST, AND WEST SIDES.

WHEN IN A BIND, A RACCOON CAN BE USED AS A HAT.

STICKS CAN BE USED TO MAKE A LEAN-TO, START A FIRE, OR MAKE ALL-NATURAL EARRINGS. BERRIES CAN BE USED FOR FOOD, BAIT, OR A NICE, SUBTLE ROUGE.

CREATIVITY IN ACTION
Discover a Hidden World!

Exploration is a key part of life. Do you remember when we discovered the lost city of Atlantis? That was a major find.

What if you could discover a previously hidden world? It doesn't have to be underwater. It could be atop a towering mountain, hidden deep in a rain forest, or under the sand of a vast, empty desert. Use the next page to draw and describe the hidden land you'd like to uncover.

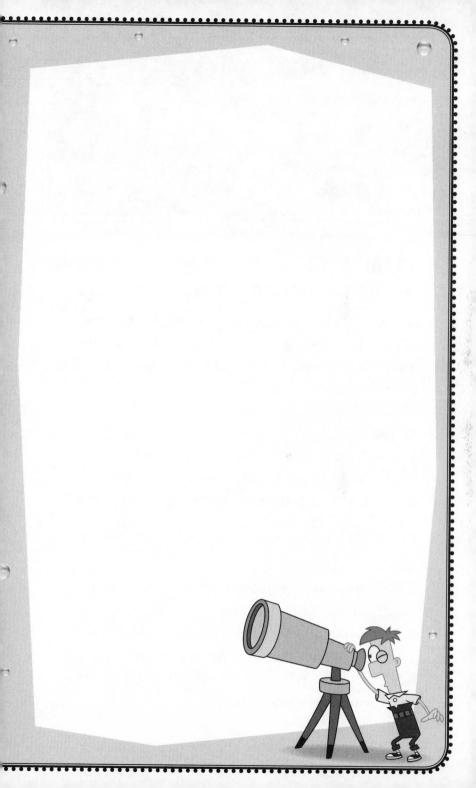

VITAL LIFE INFO
Throwing an Awesome Party

Do we even have to explain why we included this one? We love to throw a good party, so we present you with a handy list of the key factors that can take yours from so-so to totally awesome!

People

The most important element of any party is the people you invite. Try to put together an interesting mix of different types of people. We suggest astronauts, soul singers, and magicians.

Music

Second in importance to the people you invite is the music you play. We like to have a live band, a cool DJ, or Ferb, who can play the harmonica. Some of our favorite groups that always get people dancing are: Jeremy and the Incidentals, Love Handel, Bulbous Crab, and the Freeze-Dried Beat-Boxing Mommas.

Food

Pizza. Pizza. Pizza.
And nachos for Buford.

Drinks

Cider slushees.

Okay, **seriously**. Everyone loves pizza and slushees, but you need to have a balance of foods for everyone who comes to your party. We've found that the big go-to items at our gatherings are water, chips, veggie platters, and Ferb's jalapeño-cheese frittatas. Olé!

Theme

A great party needs a great theme. That will give you ideas as to how to decorate, what to wear, what the invitations should look like, and all the rest. Here are some of our favorite party themes:

- Space cowboy • Ancient Egypt • Toga
- Ugly sweater • Dress as your favorite meat product

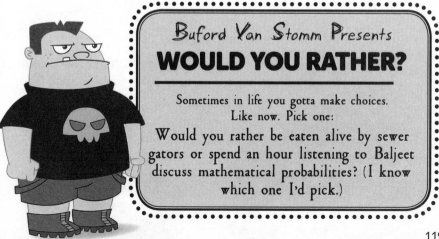

Buford Van Stomm Presents

WOULD YOU RATHER?

Sometimes in life you gotta make choices.
Like now. Pick one:

Would you rather be eaten alive by sewer gators or spend an hour listening to Baljeet discuss mathematical probabilities? (I know which one I'd pick.)

RANDOM IDEA
If We Ran the World

All the advice in this guide is based on the way things are NOW. But things could change. And they WOULD change if we ran the world.

I WOULD GIVE EVERYONE THE SUMMER OFF TO MAKE THE MOST OF EVERY DAY!

FREE ICE CREAM.

BAN INVENTIONS AND LITTLE BROTHERS.

A FEMALE MAYOR OF DANVILLE!

I'D BRING BACK BULLYING AND GIVE A PRESIDENTIAL AWARD FOR THE WORLD'S BEST WEDGIE.

WE WOULD HAVE YEAR-ROUND SCHOOL AND NO MORE BULLYING!

What would things be like if you ran the world?

....

....

What rules would you change?

....

....

What would people wear?

....

....

Eat? ....

....

Play? ....

....

Who would you pick to help you rule?

....

....

What's the biggest, most surprising change you would make?

....

....

AND NOW . . .
LIVE FROM THE HA-HA HUT!

Instructions: 1) Take out your funny bone. 2) Prepare to have it tickled.

Knock-knock!
Who's there?
Ferb.
Ferb who?

**Ferb Pete's sake,
let me in already!**

Which monster is best at dancing?

The *boogey*man!

What does Isabella say when she wants to borrow a stick of gum?

Whatcha *chewin'*?

Why did the banana have to go to the doctor's office?

It didn't peel well!

What is the first thing a platypus does in the morning?

It wakes up!

WHAT IS AT THE END OF EVERYTHING?

THE LETTER "G," OF COURSE!

QUIZ TIME
Do You Have Psychic Powers?

Everybody knows about the body's five senses—sight, hearing, touch, smell, and taste. But what about a sixth sense? A bizarre, unexplainable way of knowing something . . . or communicating something . . . or making something happen? Sometimes I know what Ferb is thinking without him even opening his mouth. In fact, that's usually the case.

Do you have a sixth sense? There's only one way to find out! (Well, actually, there's lots of ways, but this one is right in front of you.) Take this quiz!

1) **Can you sometimes read people's thoughts? What number am I thinking of right now?**

    A) 3

    B) 3.14 (Baljeet's favorite!)

    C) 17

    D) 5,385,172,351

2) **Some people can move things with their minds. Stare at a small object and concentrate on moving it for several seconds. Did it move?**

    A) Yes. Yes it did.

    B) I think so, but a tiny bit.

    C) No.

    D) It moved so far I can't find it anymore. But now there's a hole in the wall in the shape of the object. Coincidence?

3) Shuffle a deck of cards. Deal one card facedown. Don't look at it. Now stare at the back of the card until an image of the front of the card appears in your mind.

A) I did it. It only took a few seconds!

B) It took a long time, and the image was fuzzy, but I really saw the card.

C) I've been staring for hours and I really have to use the bathroom now.

D) I'm still looking for a deck of cards.

4) Sometimes, when the phone rings . . .

A) I know who is calling before I answer it.

B) I was thinking about the person on the other end right before they called.

C) I know that it's ringing, even when I'm not home! (It's called a cell phone.)

D) It's my mom telling me to do my homework.

SCORING

Give yourself one point for each time you answered A, two points for each B, three for each C, and four for each D. Then total up your score.

If you scored:

14-16: Sorry, you don't have psychic abilities, but you do have a nice personality and that counts.

11-13: You may have the beginnings of extrasensory powers! Keep working at it, and in no time you'll be an outcast.

7-10: Way to go! You're as psychic as Buford is tough.

4-6: You are completely, totally psychic. But then you knew that, didn't you?

HOW TO...
Fight a Monster

We've encountered our
fair share of monsters—and
aliens and cavemen and zombies—during our adventures.
Some of them actually became our friends, but not every
abomination is meant to be a lifelong chum (that's why
they're called monsters, after all). If you find yourself in a
situation where you have to defend yourself from a quiver-
ing gelatin monster or a marauding mummy, consult this
chart and you'll be ready to fight that fiend!

BATTLE TACTIC

	Exploit its weakness.	Lure it into a trap.	And if it comes down to hand-to-hand combat . . .
Mummy	**Scissors** *Grab a bandage and start snipping.*	**Sarcophagus** *No mummy can resist!*	Unwrap. Unwrap. Unwrap.
Vampire	**The sun** *And garlic. Get him to a sunny garlic patch, and he's toast.*	**Necks** *Vampires love necks. And necks aren't hard to find.*	Serve him a *stake* dinner.
Werewolf	**Silver** *Borrow your parents' silverware and poke him with a fork.*	**Food** *Werewolves are always hungry . . . but don't ask what they eat.*	Give him a haircut.
Frankenstein's Monster	**Fire** *But we don't advise playing with fire. Try smiling at him.*	**A female monster** *Yeah, this guy's a sucker for love.*	Unplug him.
Gelatin Monster	**Water** *A few squirt guns and a garden hose will turn this bully to goo.*	**Cafeterias** *For some reason, gelatin and cafeterias just go together.*	Eat him.

MONSTER

✦ TELL YOUR OWN STORY! ✦

Take these pictures from one of our adventures and write your own text to tell a new story!

....

....

....

....

....

....

....

FILL-IN-THE-BLANKS ADVENTURE
Robot Rampage

Go ahead! Fill in the blanks below with crazy
words to create an exciting adventure for us!

It was a .... day in Danville, and Phineas
ADJECTIVE

and Ferb were making an electromagnetic ....
NOUN

in the backyard. Ferb adjusted the dials so that it would attract

.... and repel .... But before the
PLURAL NOUN   **PLURAL NOUN**

stepbrothers could power it up, they heard a ....
ADJECTIVE

sound. *Crash! Smash!* ....! A huge robot
SOUND EFFECT

.... entered their yard. It crushed the bushes,
ADVERB

stomped the grass, and flattened the .... Where
NOUN

had it come from?

The robot was the work of the .... Dr. Heinz
ADJECTIVE

Doofenshmirtz. During a fight with Agent P, Dr. Doofenshmirtz's

.............................-inator had been accidentally activated. It
NOUN

fired a .... ray that hit the robot, sending it on its
ADJECTIVE

rampage!

But now, as Agent P battled with Dr. Doofenshmirtz atop

a ...., the misguided robot was about to
     NOUN

.... Phineas and Ferb.
   VERB

"Quick!" Phineas said. "Throw me that ....!"
                                         NOUN

Ferb threw it .... and Phineas caught it, using
                  ADVERB

it to .... the giant robot. While the robot was
     VERB

distracted, Ferb switched their electromagnetic device so that

it would repel robots. .... went the powerful
                       SOUND EFFECT

magnetic pulse!

Repelled by Phineas and Ferb's device, the mighty robot

turned and ran away like a ...., never to be
                            NOUN

seen again.

"Well, that was ....," Phineas said with
                 ADJECTIVE

a sigh.

"Yes," Ferb replied. "I guess that's why they call giant

robots the .... of ....!"
           NOUN   **PLACE**

RANDOM ADVICE
Never Annoy a Wildebeest

. . . and other hard-won
pieces of invaluable advice!

Some tips defy categorization. That means they don't
fit well into any of our other lists. But they are no less
important! So if you take to heart any part of our guide to
life, please, please, please make it these vital tips.

▶ Don't challenge huge professional wrestlers. They hate
to lose.

▶ Construction sites and old, dilapidated amusement
parks put up those signs that say DANGER! KEEP OUT! for
a reason.

▶ Never annoy a wildebeest. Let's just say they have tempers.

▶ Think twice before detonating . . . anything.

▶ Not all heavyset men with beards are Santa. Or jolly.

FINISH YOUR OWN COMIC!

HOW TO...
Scale an Active Volcano

When we were in Hawaii on vacation, Candace asked us to help her climb to the top of an ancient volcano. We were happy to help, but she didn't seem to know the first thing about volcano scaling. So we compiled a list of things you should keep in mind if you ever attempt to climb a volcano.

Five Things to NEVER Do While Ascending a Lava-Filled Peak!

1) Don't touch the red stuff. That bubbling, oozing, glowing liquid is called lava or magma. It's extremely hot and has a tendency to melt everything in its path . . . including you.

2) Don't go barefoot. Volcanoes are formed when the lava hardens into sharp, pointy rocks. Feet don't like sharp, pointy rocks, and sharp, pointy rocks don't like feet.

3) Don't spit into the wind. This isn't limited to volcano climbing. It's just a good rule wherever you are.

4) Don't forget your climbing gear. Any climb requires safety gear, such as ropes and helmets, but it's extra important when you're heading up something that can start shaking like a mechanical bull at any second.

5) Don't forget your platypus. Hey, that reminds us, where's Perry?

WRITE YOUR OWN ADVICE!

You've read through almost an entire book of our advice. But now we're curious about *your* advice! What have you learned from your time on planet Earth that is essential for other people to know? If you could only pass on three tips, what would they be?

TIP #1 ....

....

....

....

TIP #2 ....

....

....

....

And most importantly,

TIP #3 ....

....

....

....

....

....

DESIGN CHALLENGE
Finish Ferb's Blueprints

Ferb got interrupted before he could finish the blueprints for his latest invention. Can you complete the plans and turn this into our coolest project yet?

Ferb's Take

FERB'S LIST OF TEN THINGS YOU MUST DO IN YOUR LIFETIME

This one's self-explanatory, really. And here they are:

1) Surprise everyone and do something impossible. Just because they say it can't be done, it doesn't mean they're right!

2) Bake cupcakes for a llama. Hey, the poor guy can't do it himself.

3) Be the first person in your family to visit a foreign land. Like the Antarctic. Or Neptune. Or that new deli down the street.

4) Enter a beauty contest . . . underwater!

5) Tightrope-walk across the Grand Canyon. Just to be safe, get a really big net.

6) Write a book. (Like we just did! Although yours should probably have a different title so people don't get confused.)

7) Create something no one has ever seen before. Swimming fins for an ostrich. A bed that makes itself. Antimatter.

8) Visit a local museum, and then re-create your favorite exhibit. We liked one we saw about ancient Greece, so we devised a whole chariot race!

9) Learn to like vegetables. You'll be glad you did when they rise up and take over the world.

10) Enjoy time under a tree with your best friend.

GUIDE TO YOUR FUTURE

Well, throughout this book we've given you a lot of tips and advice on things you may encounter in your life. But how can you know exactly what the future holds? Will you be disgustingly rich? A crazed beautician with a pet lizard? Is there any way to know for sure?

Now there is, with our amazing **GUIDE TO YOUR FUTURE**. Here's how it works. Pick four numbers between 1 and 10 and write them below.

YOUR FUTURE!

....

YOUR SECOND LIFE!

....

THIRD TIME'S THE CHARM!

....

Good! Now take the first number you wrote and count down that many rows from the top of COLUMN A on the next page. Write down whatever you find there in the first blank on page 143. Take the second number you wrote and count down that many rows from the top of COLUMN B on the next page. Write down whatever you find there in the second blank on page 143. Do the same for the third and fourth numbers you picked! And so on . . .

COLUMN A

- Deliriously happy
- Paranoid
- Strong and healthy
- Beyond famous
- Very stinky
- Highly dangerous
- Disgustingly wealthy
- Rapidly expanding
- Grumpy but lovable
- Fascinatingly odd

COLUMN B

- Mad scientist
- Minimum-wage cartoonist
- Coal miner
- Unpaid intern (like Carl!)
- Crab fisherman
- Action star
- Hobo
- Multimillionaire
- Trained baboon
- Antiques dealer (like our dad!)

COLUMN C

- Seventeen and a half kids
- A giant wolfhound named Hans
- A gorgeous spouse from Brazil
- More friends than you can handle
- Baljeet
- A crew of pirates at your command
- Seventy-eight relatives crashing at your place
- A tall, dark stranger
- A house full of needy cats
- A robot named Norm

COLUMN D

- An obsession with busting your brothers
- A lot of speeding tickets
- A black belt in karate
- A direct connection to alien life forms
- A tendency to bully
- A deathly fear of musicals
- A love for Phineas
- A lifetime supply of bubble gum
- A summer home in Gimmelshtump
- A love/hate relationship with egg salad

Now tremble in awe as Phineas and Ferb's guide to your future spells out the unforeseen events yet to come!

YOUR FUTURE!

The mystical energies tell us that you will be a ....
COLUMN A

.... with .... and ....
COLUMN B   COLUMN C   COLUMN D

That is your future. Phineas and Ferb have spoken!

YOUR SECOND LIFE!

If that doesn't work out for you, the mystical energies tell us

that you will be a .... with
COLUMN A   COLUMN B

.... and .... That is your second life.
COLUMN C   COLUMN D

Phineas and Ferb have spoken!

THIRD TIME'S THE CHARM!

And if you're still not satisfied, our crystal ball tells us that you will

be a .... with ....
COLUMN A   COLUMN B   COLUMN C

and .... Enough! Phineas and Ferb have spoken!
COLUMN D

~~~~~~ **CONCLUSION** ~~~~~~

Hey, guys! Thanks for reading our guide to life . . . and for giving us your advice, too. We liked writing this book and hope you enjoyed reading it!

If we can give you one more tip before we go, it would be this:

There's no such thing as an ordinary day . . . so make the most of every one!

Oh, and don't forget to floss.

See ya,

Phineas & FERB